The Tiger and the Wise Man

Andrew Fusek Peters

illustrated by
Diana Mayo

Published by Child's Play (International) Ltd
Swindon   Auburn ME   Sydney

Text © 2004 A. Fusek Peters   Illustrations © 2004 Child's Play (International) Ltd
ISBN 978-1-904550-07-5   www.childs-play.com   Printed in China
3 5 7 9 10 8 6 4 2

Tiger was being very badly behaved as usual.
In fact, he was asking for trouble, what with terrifying toddlers,
chasing children and being totally beastly to all the other animals
at the watering hole.

"Enough is enough!" cried the villagers.
"We must teach that tiresome tiger a lesson!"
So, they gathered together to build a cage out of bamboo,
hid it in a bush, and put a nice tempting lump of meat inside.

Oh what a smell! Tiger's tummy trembled.
He purred with anticipation. He was so entranced,
he padded straight into that cage, and WHOOOMP!
Down came the door! Tiger was trapped!

"Ha! Serves you right!"
laughed the villagers,
as they danced off
to hold a feast in celebration
of the BIG CAT IN A CAGE.

Along came a wise man, who had
no idea what a nuisance Tiger
had been. He paused by the cage.

"Oh, Mr Wise Man!
Oh, Me! Oh, My!" Tiger moaned.
He made one of his paws look
injured, and he panted pathetically
as if he were ill.

"How can I be of help, Mr Tiger?"
asked the wise man.
"I have been tricked and trapped
by the terrible villagers,"
whined the tiger. "They want
to turn me into a rug!
Please, please let me out!"

"Let you out?"
laughed the wise man.
"That would be very un-wise.
You'll simply eat me up!"

"Eat you?" grimaced the tiger.
He looked closely at the tasty
man-sized morsel.
He would be perfect
for his breakfast! "I promise!"

"Oh, well, that's all right then. I take you at your word, good Tiger!"
The wise man smiled, and opened the cage door.
Tiger sprang out as quickly as a catapult, and grabbed
the wise man in his sharp jaws.

"But you made a promise!" wailed the wise man.
"To eat you! Yes! Indeed I did. You should
have listened more closely to what I said.
Now please don't make any more noise,
or you will put me off my breakfast!"
Tiger opened his jaws wide.
He drooled. He dribbled.
He had awful table manners,
very meaty breath, and
his teeth were far too sharp
for the wise man's liking.

The wise man thought very quickly. He had no desire
to take a trip to Tiger's tummy.

"Just wait a second, Tiger!" announced the wise man.
"What is it? I haven't got all day!"
growled the tiger, grumpily picking his teeth.

"I want a second opinion on this!" the wise man demanded.
"It really is not fair that I let you out of the cage,
just so that you can turn around and swallow me!"

"Well, you might be right," agreed the tiger, peevishly.
"All right then. I suppose I can wait for my breakfast
a little longer."

Tiger held firmly onto
the wise man, and together
they approached the Banyan
Tree to ask for her opinion:
Should the tiger eat the wise man?

"Hmmmn!" rumbled the big old Banyan.
"Well, it is very pleasant when people seek
my shade by day, and in the twilight, poets are
inspired by my beauty. Yet, after dark, my branches
and my sisters' branches are cut down for firewood
and fancy furniture, and my leaves are stripped bare!"

Banyan began to shake
with anger. "The human race
is beyond be-leaf!

So I say,
Let the tiger eat the wise man!"

"That's settled then!" announced the tiger.
"My belly is rumbling and..."

"Be patient!   Let me ask for another opinion," pleaded
the wise man, who very much wanted to carry on breathing.

"Oh, really, this is too much!" sighed the tiger. "Come on then, Lunch-on-Legs! Let's be quick about it!" So, off they set to look for Crocodile on the bank of the river. The wise man stepped up onto a long, green log to get a better view.

"Oi!" snapped Crocodile, throwing the wise man into a slimy mud bath. "What do you want? I was just in the middle of a nice snooze!" Tiger hurriedly put the question to him.

"Hmmmn...!" said the Crocodile, in a slithery voice. "You human beings are always chasing me with your big guns! And what for, a pair of shoes? You humans get under my skin!" he hissed through sharp teeth.

"So, I say, Let the tiger eat the wise man!" With that, Crocodile slipped away into the river.

"My opinion precisely!" smiled the tiger. "And not before time.
You started off as breakfast, and now you will have to be lunch!
Just a sprinkling of salt, with some toasted coriander, to make you tastier..."

"Just you wait a minute,
you big hairy bully!"
snivelled the wise man.
"I am not ready for serving up yet!"

He pointed to Eagle soaring through the hot afternoon.

"A last opinion! Just one more!" he cried. Tiger hissed
in irritation, as Eagle landed gracefully on a nearby branch.

"More delays!
What a waste of valuable munch-time,"
growled Tiger, as he grudgingly
asked Eagle for her opinion.

"Hmmm...." screeched the Eagle.
"I am Queen of the Sky,
Rajah of the Blue Heavens.
Up here, only the wind can do battle
with me.

But when I nest, humans come
and steal my eggs. They shoot at me
and stuff me and stick me on their walls
to show off!" She fixed the wise man
with a beady eye:

"So I say, Let the tiger eat the wise man!"

Eagle flew off, and the tiger turned with a smile to the wise man. "No more excuses! It's already dinner time! Maybe I should toast you a little first?" He tapped his sharp claws impatiently.

The wise man gave up all hope. "Do what you like!" he cried. "Toast, boil or casserole, my life is not worth a fig!"

With that, he flung himself at the mercy of the snarling beast, face down, with his hands over his ears so that he would not have to hear the tiger's reply.

At that very moment, a jackal came sauntering by.
She had overheard the whole conversation. "My dear Tiger.
What a clever fellow you are!" she barked, in a flattering tone.

"Do you think so?" Tiger puffed up his chest with pride.
"Oh yes, indeed. You really are the King of the Cats!"
"Oh, well, it was nothing really!" the tiger preened.
"But tell me," asked the jackal, looking fascinated,
"Where is the cage you managed to escape from?"

Tiger was more than happy to tell the story.
He even padded back to the bush where the cage was hidden,
leaving the wise man where he lay.

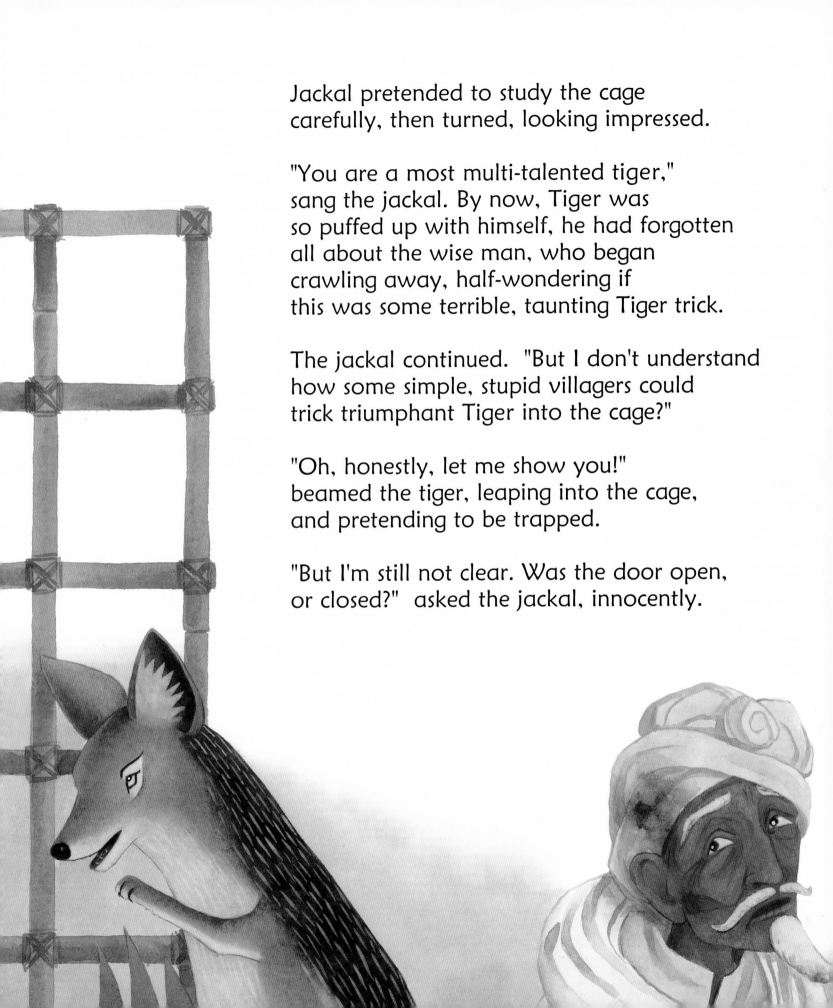

Jackal pretended to study the cage
carefully, then turned, looking impressed.

"You are a most multi-talented tiger,"
sang the jackal. By now, Tiger was
so puffed up with himself, he had forgotten
all about the wise man, who began
crawling away, half-wondering if
this was some terrible, taunting Tiger trick.

The jackal continued. "But I don't understand
how some simple, stupid villagers could
trick triumphant Tiger into the cage?"

"Oh, honestly, let me show you!"
beamed the tiger, leaping into the cage,
and pretending to be trapped.

"But I'm still not clear. Was the door open,
or closed?" asked the jackal, innocently.

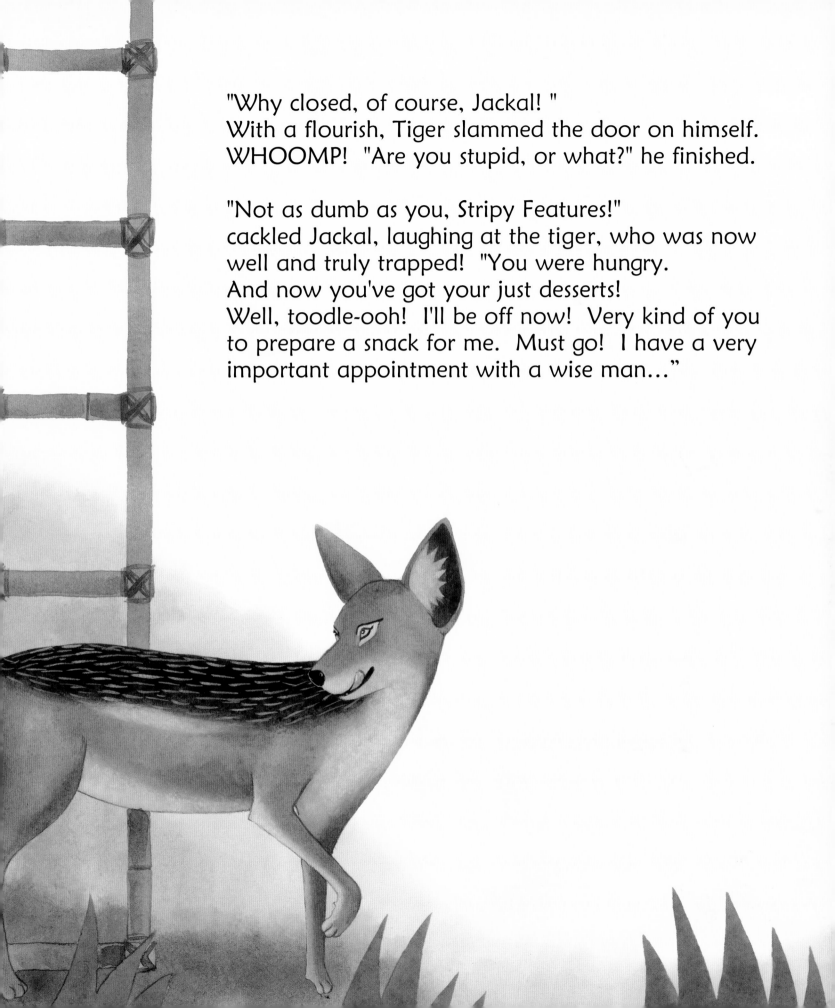

"Why closed, of course, Jackal! "
With a flourish, Tiger slammed the door on himself.
WHOOMP! "Are you stupid, or what?" he finished.

"Not as dumb as you, Stripy Features!"
cackled Jackal, laughing at the tiger, who was now
well and truly trapped! "You were hungry.
And now you've got your just desserts!
Well, toodle-ooh! I'll be off now! Very kind of you
to prepare a snack for me. Must go! I have a very
important appointment with a wise man..."

Jackal trotted off, sniggering to herself.
All that cleverness had made her horribly hungry.

"Coooooo-eeee, Mr Wise Man! Don't run away!"
she called, licking her lips.
"You haven't thanked me for tricking Tiger!
As a reward, how about treating me to...

...DINNER!"